WHO IS MAJOR ROB?

as told by **Mr. SOCKS**

Written by **PAUL R. FESSOCK** Illustrated by **YOLANDA V. FUNDORA**

For My Four Rockers, All the best!:
Jessica, Ella, Natalie and Juliet

To My Mom (Mama Leo):
For all the unwavering support every time, every day! Thank you!

To My Second Parents , Gary and Barbara Benko:
Thanks for all the advice throughout the years!

To General Whittington:
Who first answered the call when my brother needed help.
I'll never forget. Thank you!

To Catch A Lift (CAL):
For helping my brother and many more veterans get back on their
feet through fitness and friendship. Thank you!

In Memory

Major Robert J. Marchanti

Corporal Chris Coffland

For permission contact: Paul@worldofrockmusic.com

Published by World of Rock Publishing.

Visit us online at: www.mrsocksworldofrock.com

**Illustrations and book design by
Yolanda V. Fundora / www.TowardADigitalAesthetic.com**

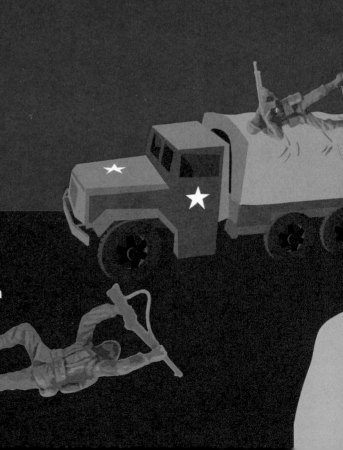

Who is Major Rob?

It's very easy to remember.

One late winter,
he became our newest
family member.

He was not called
Major Rob at first.
That's a title
that he earned.

Turn to page 29
to learn about the
Bronze Star.

Bronze
Star

Rob loved to get dirty
and do his own thing.
He loved to play rough,
and he also loved to sing.

7

But playing with our army trucks and soldiers is what we always did.

I remember that especially from when I was a kid.

We played
all kinds
of sports
and learned
to play
instruments.

We were so very
lucky to have
supportive
parents.

9

When high school ended
college was the way to go.

He graduated with a degree and became a 2nd Lieutenant in the Army.

We were all very proud and threw him a party.

My dad would say, "Party time is over,
now the real work will begin.
By serving your country
with honor, you will always win."

When we were young,
playing soldier
was exciting,
but in real life, people
get hurt when fighting.

Rob and his unit
were always
on alert.
Sometimes he saw
his friends
and other
people get hurt.

They always heard
loud noises
and things
that went "boom!"
in the night.

His buddies were always by his side
and that made him feel all right.

Rob's deployment was over, and he made it back safe and sound.

20

Sometimes, he would laugh a lot, and then we would see him cry. One day, we were at a store, and for no reason, he yelled at a guy.

I contacted someone Rob looked up to and admired. General Whittington was good at getting his soldiers to feel inspired.

The General jumped into action and had a special doctor talk to Rob. He was diagnosed with Post Traumatic Stress Disorder (PTSD), a mental health condition soldiers sometimes get on the job.

Turn to page 29 and learn about PTSD.

Rob was treated with medication,
and he learned strategies to obtain relaxation.

Those methods worked, but what caught my
attention were his friends
at this new organization.

The group was called Catch A Lift, and they gave him purpose realistically.

They help get veterans get back into shape both physically and mentally.

Lynn, Adam and her team gave Rob their friendship in his time of need.

In life, all you have to do is listen.
That alone can help anyone in a tough position.

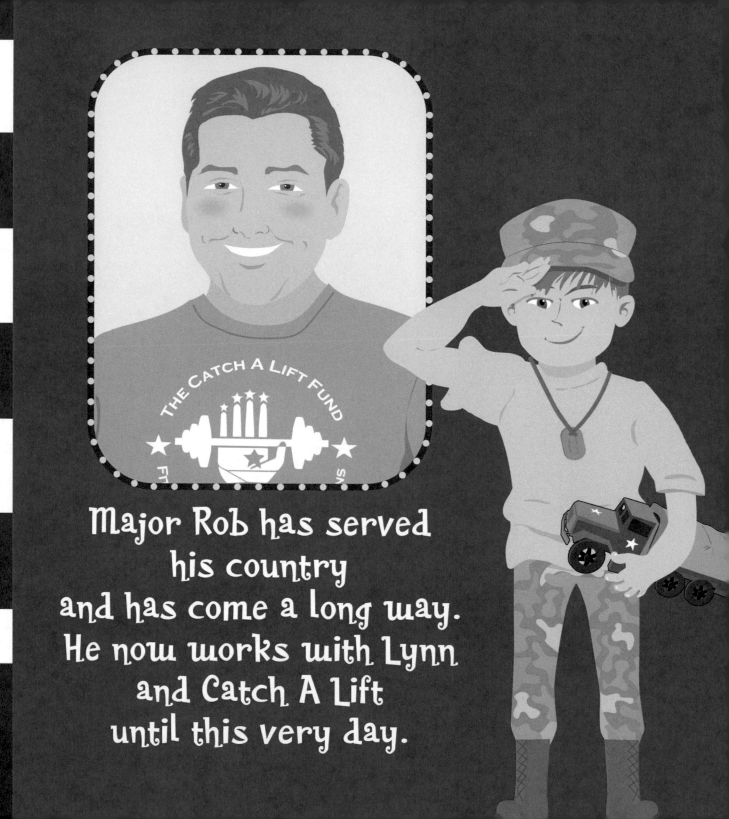

Major Rob has served
his country
and has come a long way.
He now works with Lynn
and Catch A Lift
until this very day.

BRONZE STAR

The Bronze Star Medal is a United States decoration awarded to members of the United States Armed Forces for either heroic achievement, heroic service, admirable achievement, or praiseworthy service in a combat zone.

POST TRAUMATIC STRESS DISORDER (PTSD)

Post-traumatic Stress can occur following a life-threatening event like military combat, natural disasters and serious accidents. People who suffer from PTSD often suffer from nightmares, flashbacks, difficulty sleeping, and feeling emotionally drained. Members of the military exposed to war/combat and other groups at high risk for trauma exposure are at risk for developing PTSD.

This guy is for real!

Major Rob Fessock grew up in South Plainfield, New Jersey. He graduated from South Plainfield High School in 1993. Major Rob graduated from Towson University in 1998, and received his commission as a Second Lieutenant in the United States Army through the Reserve Officer Training Corps (ROTC). In 2007, he served in Iraq, and supported Operation Iraqi Freedom with the 58th Infantry Brigade Combat Team. Major Rob was also deployed to Afghanistan in 2011, and supported Operation Enduring Freedom with the 29th Infantry Division. Rob currently volunteers with the Catch A Lift Fund in Baltimore, Maryland, a nationwide 501C3 non-profit wellness platform for combat wounded veterans to help them heal mind, body, and spirit.

MAJOR ROB WOULD LIKE TO THANK:
Major General Charles Whittington, Brigadier General Robert Frick, Colonel James Shelby, Lieutenant Colonel George Downey, Lieutenant Colonel Robert Puleo, Master Sergeant Ken McGill, First Sergeant John Fitzgibbons, Sergeant First Class Mike Cunningham, Sergeant First Class Russell Myers, Staff Sergeant Ken Kincaid, Lynn Coffland, Catch A Lift Staff, Adam Vengrow, Andrew Berman, Keith Veltre and Family, Leonor Fessock (Mom) and Paul R Fessock (Mr. Socks).

For more information, please visit
www.catchaliftfund.org

Paul R. Fessock is a teacher of physical education at Brayton Elementary School in Summit, NJ and has been for over 20 years. He emphasizes social-emotional well-being through fitness and play.

Paul has created his own entertainment enterprise for children: *World of Rock Music Lessons and More* and *Mr. Socks' World of Rock*, a channel on Youtube that inspires children to love music. Paul attended Towson University in Maryland. He and his wife, Jessica, an elementary school supervisor, reside in Scotch Plains, NJ with their three children, Ella, Natalie and Juliet.

This is Paul's third children's book in the *Who Is* series. The first two books are **Who is Johnny One Lipp?** and **Who is Heavy Metal Harry?**

Visit us online at: www.mrsocksworldofrock.com

www.whoisjohnnyonelipp.com   www.worldofrockmusic.com

Yolanda V. Fundora is a Cuban-American fine artist, textile, book designer, and book illustrator.

She most recently published a fine art book, *I Have a Car Who Likes to Wear Hats (and other visual tales)*. Other fine art books include *Toward A Digital Aesthetic: the Art of Yolanda V. Fundora.* and *A Garden Alphabetized (for your viewing pleasure)*.

You can see her work at www.TowardADigitalAesthetic.com.

Founded in memory of Army Cpl. Chris Coffland, Catch A Lift Fund (CAL) enables post 911 combat wounded Veterans to regain and maintain their physical and mental health by providing granted gym memberships, fitness programs or in-home gym equipment, anywhere in the United States.

A portion of the proceeds from **Who is Major Rob?** will go to the Catch A Lift Fund.

To find out more: www.catchaliftfund.com

Made in the USA
Coppell, TX
30 October 2022